There's a
KANGAROO
in My Soup!

There's a KANGAROO in My Soup!

Joan Lennon

Illustrated by Wendy Rasmussen

Front Street / Cricket Books
Chicago

Library of Congress Cataloging-in-Publication Data
Lennon, Joan.
    There's a kangaroo in my soup! / Joan Lennon ; illustrated by Wendy Rasmussen.—1st ed.
        p. cm.
    Summary: When Cynthia the boisterous kangaroo runs away from the circus, she hides
    out at quiet Kevin's house and helps him solve the mystery surrounding his parents' inventions.
    ISBN 0-8126-2898-5
    [1. Kangaroos—Fiction. 2. Jokes—Fiction. 3. Inventions—Fiction. 4. Mystery and
    detective stories.] I. Rasmussen, Wendy, ill. II. Title.
    PZ7.L5393 Th 2000
    [Fic]—dc21

                                                                            00-037141

To the happy memory of my father
—J. L.

To my father, Torben, who passed
on the artistic gene, and to my
husband, John, for putting up
with the results
—W. R.

Contents

CHAPTER 1

Something Has Got to Change!

Kevin was a quiet boy. He lived in a quiet house, on a quiet street, in a quiet town. *Nothing* exciting had ever happened to him.

Kevin's mom and dad were inventors. They invented things in a shed in their backyard. You'd have thought that was exciting, and it *should* have been, but it wasn't, because the things they invented never got made. As soon as Kevin's mom and dad thought of something, and drew pictures of it, and had conversations at breakfast about "where to put the sprocket pocket" or "adding bits that go *blarp*," then, sure as anything, somebody else started selling the very same thing in the stores. For lots of money.

Kevin's mom and dad got sadder and sadder. They also got poorer and poorer. And Kevin got quieter and quieter.

It was getting so bad that Kevin's mom and dad started to think they should stop inventing and get real jobs instead.

"And there *are* real jobs around," said Kevin's mom, trying to sound cheerful. "The Blue Begonia is looking for another waitress, and the Everything and Then Some Department Store has a sign out for a new cleaner."

"And Mrs. Stopper, the crossing guard at school, may be retiring soon," said Kevin, trying to sound cheerful. "Her feet are getting worse."

"There you are!" said Kevin's dad, trying

to sound cheerful, too. "A perfect job for me! I'd make a great crossing guard!"

Then he sighed.

It was very depressing.

It was so depressing that Kevin began to dread the times when his teacher ran out of things to teach and asked them what-they-wanted-to-be-when-they-grew-up. It was hard to say, "I want to be a great inventor like my mom and dad," because nobody at school thought Kevin's mom and dad *were* great. Some of the kids looked as if they were sorry for him, and some of them laughed behind their hands, but it was obvious that nobody thought, I wish *my* mom and dad did amazing stuff like that. They probably just looked at his jacket, which was getting too small for him again, and thought, Why don't Kevin's parents get *real* jobs?

As Kevin walked home from school one Tuesday afternoon, he was thinking sad thoughts.

This is awful, he thought. This can't go on. Something has *got* to change!

And you know, he was right. . . .

CHAPTER 2

The Circus
Leaves Town

On the other side of town, a circus was packing up.

"O.K.," said the Ringmaster grumpily. "Fred the Strongman and Marlene the Twisty Lady take the first van. Mystic Doris, you take the second van with the Ringing Brothers. I'll take the last van with Cynthia."

"Uh, Boss?" said Reg, the youngest Ringing Brother. "Cynthia ain't here, Boss. Uh, she's gone."

"Gone?"

"Yeah. Gone."

"What?! And all the costumes?"

Reg gulped nervously and nodded.

There was a short silence while the Ringmaster's face slowly turned the color of a red brick house.

"She won't get away with this!" he hissed. "We've got a show coming up next week in Twotowns Over, and she's on the bill. You, Twisty Lady, I want you to stay behind here. You find her. Do whatever it takes. Keep the Strongman with you in case you need muscle. Get going!"

"But, Boss," whined Fred the Strongman, "it's getting late! I haven't had my supper! You *know* I go all wobbly if I don't eat regular."

The Twisty Lady nodded.

The Ringmaster started to argue, then changed his mind.

"Oh, all right," he said grudgingly. "But first thing after supper, got it? I want her found, and I want her back. I'll

collect you—and her—in town at twelve noon Friday, and not a second later!"

He jerked his head at the others.

"Let's go."

Doris, the Ringmaster, Reg, and the others headed for the vans that were leaving. Marlene and Fred climbed into the remaining van to get on with supper before the Strongman wobbled.

And, waiting to be discovered, a trail of strange footprints could be seen in the mud, leading toward town. Very strange footprints indeed . . .

CHAPTER 3

Introducing the Morning Glory Machine

That evening, Kevin and his mom and dad were sitting quietly in the kitchen. Kevin was finishing his homework, and his parents were looking over the plans for their latest invention.

"This is it, Kevin," said his dad. "Our last try. If we can't succeed with this, then it's hello to real jobs for us!"

"Have a look, dear," said his mom shyly. "I think it might be our best yet."

She pushed the pile of papers over to Kevin, and he looked. Then he grinned. And his grin got bigger. AND BIGGER!

"Wow!" said Kevin.

It was absolutely and utterly amazing.

The invention was called the Morning Glory Machine, and once it was built, it would change the face of mornings forever. It was a machine that could—

get you washed

comb your hair

hand you your clothes (one at a time),
  making sure your underpants were
  the right way around

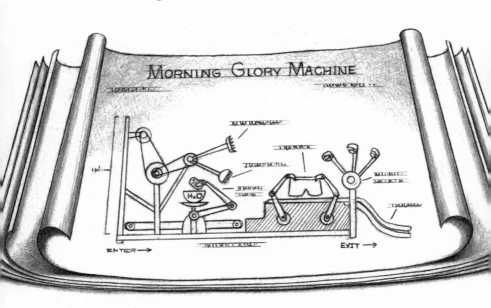

put your homework in your book bag
remember your lunch money
and tie your shoes.

With a Morning Glory Machine, you could be out the door and halfway to school without ever properly waking up, and *still* be fully dressed (including underpants the right way around) *and* have everything you needed. The only thing it couldn't do was eat your breakfast for you, but Kevin's mom and dad were working on that.

Kevin was thinking how brilliant his parents were, when the doorbell rang.

"Answer that, would you, dear?" said Kevin's mom, reaching for the plans.

"O.K., Mom," said Kevin.

He went to open the front door and was just about to say, "Hello?" when something large and furry jumped in, knocked him over, and sat on him.

"Save me, save me!" gasped the thing.

"*They're after me! Help, help! Pleeeease,
you MUST save me*—actually, you don't
have to save me, but, well, it would be
very nice if you would."

"Er," said Kevin.

"I'll take that as a yes," said the thing. "Which bedroom is yours?"

"Upstairs. On the right," said Kevin. "Er, you're squishing me."

"You're welcome," said the thing, and before Kevin knew what was happening, it had jumped off him and disappeared up the stairs.

Kevin lay on the floor for a bit. Then he got up and went back into the kitchen.

"Who wath ith? Wong houth?" asked his dad fuzzily. He had a pencil in his mouth.

"I'm not sure," said Kevin in a puzzled voice.

His mom looked up from the plans. "Are you all right?" she asked.

Kevin gave himself a shake and smiled at her. "Sure," he said.

His mom smiled, too, and turned back to the plans.

After a minute, Kevin said, "I think I'll go upstairs now."

"That's nice, dear," said Kevin's parents.

CHAPTER 4

Mistress of a Thousand Disguises

Kevin walked upstairs. He went to the bathroom and brushed his teeth.

"Just my imagination," he said to himself in the bathroom mirror.

In the hall, he stopped to look at a picture of a lake and some trees.

"Don't be silly," he said to the picture.

He went to the door of his bedroom and looked at the doorknob.

"I'll just go into my empty bedroom now," he said to the doorknob.

Nothing happened.

"This is me, going in," he said after a while.

Nothing happened again.

"Oh, for goodness sake!" said Kevin at last and opened the door.

He walked straight in and came as close to fainting as you're ever likely to come without dialing 911.

For there, standing in the corner, by the window, was a huge furry thing with a lampshade on its head.

"What . . . who are you?" croaked Kevin.

The thing began to hum.

"Hum, hum, hum," it said. "I'm just a lamp. Hum, hum. Eat electricity, I do, give off light. Hum."

There was a pause.

"You aren't, you know," said Kevin quite bravely. "You're that thing. From downstairs. In fact, I think you're a kangaroo."

The lampshade tilted, and a long furry face peeked out.

"Wow!" it said admiringly. "You're great! My disguises have fooled thousands. But not you! Wow!"

Kevin blushed.

"Er, thank you. I'm Kevin."

The kangaroo leaped at him, one paw stuck out.

"Cynthia. Glad to know you. My card."

Kevin had leaped back nervously, but now he took the card and read—

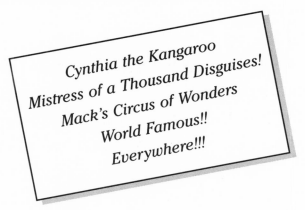

Cynthia the Kangaroo
Mistress of a Thousand Disguises!
Mack's Circus of Wonders
World Famous!!
Everywhere!!!

"A thousand disguises?" said Kevin.

"Ta-da!" said Cynthia, pointing with both paws to a small suitcase.

"In *there?*" asked Kevin.

Cynthia nodded.

"You just have to know how to fold things right," she said.

It was Kevin's turn to look admiring. But then he frowned.

"But . . . ," he said. "What circus? Where . . . ? Why . . . ?"

"I've escaped!" whispered Cynthia dramatically, making her big eyes even bigger. "I've escaped from the circus to follow my true calling!"

"Your . . . ?" asked Kevin.

"Stand-up comic," said Cynthia. "I tell kangaroo jokes. It's all I've ever wanted to do, but the Ringmaster would never let me. 'You're on the bill,' he always said. 'Disguises is what it says, and disguises is what you'll do.'"

She shook her head sadly, and her ears drooped.

Kevin was afraid Cynthia might burst into tears at any moment, so he said the first thing that came into his mind.

"Kangaroo jokes? Could you tell me one? Please?"

There was an immediate change in Cynthia. Her eyes brightened. Her enormous ears perked up. The suitcase clicked open. "Disguise Number 632," she whispered over her shoulder to Kevin. Then Cynthia, wearing a funny hat and a red nose, leaped into the middle of the room.

"What do you do with a nearsighted kangaroo?"

"Um . . . ," said Kevin.

"Take her to the hoptician. BOOM-BOOM!"

Cynthia looked at Kevin expectantly.

Kevin giggled, then said, "Er." But she was off again.

"What do you give kangaroos when they're sick?"

"I don't know," said Kevin.

"A hoperation. BOOM-BOOM!"

"Boom-boom?" said Kevin. "Why do you say 'boom-boom'?"

Cynthia stopped. "That's the drummer," she said. "You tell the joke, the drummer goes *boom-boom,* and then the people know it's time to laugh."

"That's great!" said Kevin.

Cynthia bounced onto the bed beside him and grinned.

Kevin thought for a minute, and then he said, "You know, you remind me of my mom and dad. Except . . . opposite. I mean, you had a job you didn't like, and now you're going to do a job you *do* like. And my mom and dad have a job they really, really like, and now . . . it looks like . . . unless they can . . ."

Kevin gulped and stopped.

"Tell me," said Cynthia kindly.

Kevin took one look into the kangaroo's big brown eyes under the funny hat and behind the red nose, and decided to do just that.

CHAPTER 5

The Plot Thickens

Kevin told Cynthia all about his parents and their bad luck with inventions and all the talk about getting real jobs.

Cynthia snorted.

"Bad luck?" she said. "Sounds more like a thief to me."

Kevin stared. It had never occurred to him that somebody might be *stealing* his parents' ideas.

"Oh yes," said Cynthia. "I'm always right about things like this. Mark my words, there's a thief all right. Now, tell me, have you noticed any suspicious characters hanging around?"

"Well," said Kevin slowly, thinking hard. "There's Officer MacAngus. He walks down our street most days. But that's not because he's a suspicious character. He just likes being where it's quiet, and he says our street's the quietest beat in town."

Cynthia nodded reluctantly.

"Not suspicious," she agreed. "Who else?"

"Well," said Kevin, "there's Jonathan, the paperboy. But, of course, delivering papers isn't very suspicious, either . . . is it?" He looked at Cynthia. She was tapping the side of her nose with one claw and looking wise.

"Tell me," she said. "Does this so-called Jonathan always deliver the right paper?"

"Uh, yes," said Kevin, confused.

"I thought as much." Cynthia nodded wisely. "Doesn't sound like a real paperboy

to *me*. Sounds like Suspect Number 1!"
And she held up one paw.

"Wow!" said Kevin.

"Who else?" asked Cynthia.

"Well, there's Mrs. Trott," said Kevin.
"She's a little old lady who walks her
dogs past here twice a day. But she
doesn't hang around, you know. She's
really small, and the dogs
are really
big. Nothing
suspicious
there . . . ?"

But Cynthia knew better.

"Think about it," she said. "Little old lady . . . great big dogs . . . smells fishy to me. She could very well be a spy for an invention factory, just *pretending* to be little and old. I suggest we have Suspect Number 2!" And she held up her other paw. Then she looked expectantly at Kevin.

"That's about it," he said apologetically.

There was a pause.

"Except . . . ," Kevin said.

Cynthia's ears perked up.

"Except?"

"Except for the Double-Pane Salesman."

"The what?" said Cynthia.

"Just a man," said Kevin. "He comes around to our house every little while to see if we want to buy double-pane windows. It's weird, the way he keeps coming, even when we always say no. My mom thinks he's creepy. But I guess it's just his job." Kevin shrugged. "Suspect Number 3?" he said.

Cynthia looked doubtful, then grinned.

"No stone unturned!" she agreed cheerfully. "And, now, to work!"

She leaped across the room, rummaged in her suitcase, and whirled around.

She was wearing a Sherlock Holmes hat and cape with a Sherlock Holmes pipe stuck between her large teeth.

"Ta-da!" she said, and the pipe fell out. "Disguise Number 28½! Kevin, my dear boy, the plot thickens!"

"Wow!" said Kevin. "So what happens now?"

"First," said Cynthia, "we shadow the suspects."

Kevin looked puzzled.

"You know," explained the kangaroo, "follow them about. Find out about *them* without them finding out about *us*. Tail them."

Kevin grinned shyly.

"You'd be good at that," he said.

There was a moment of puzzled silence. Then—

"Boom-boom?" said Kevin.

Cynthia looked at Kevin (who was slowly turning pink). Then she looked over her shoulder at a kangaroo's pride and joy. She looked at Kevin again.

Then she laughed. And laughed. Which made Kevin laugh. Which made *her* laugh even more.

It's a wonderful feeling, your first successful joke.

CHAPTER 6

Fred and the Twisty Lady on the Trail

Officer MacAngus strolled contentedly down the quiet street. He was a happy man, patrolling his favorite part of town on a quiet Tuesday evening.

But the sound of loud, sudden laughter coming from one of the houses did *not* make him happy.

"I say, I say. Don't like that," he muttered to himself. "Like it quiet, I do."

He stopped, put his hands on his hips, and frowned hard at the house.

He was frowning so hard, he didn't notice a shadowy figure creeping around

from the backyard with a briefcase under its arm.

He didn't notice the strange footprints that led up to the front door.

And he didn't notice Fred and Marlene, coming up the street behind him, following the trail of footprints like a pair of unlikely bloodhounds.

The laughter died away, and Officer MacAngus strolled on down the street.

But for some reason he did not understand, Officer MacAngus felt strangely ill at ease.

● ● ● ● ● ● ● ● ●

"Right," whispered Marlene. "She's hiding in there."

"So what do we do now?" whispered the Strongman.

"We go and listen outside every window until we hear her voice, of course."

"What if she's not talking?" asked the Strongman.

The Twisty Lady made a rude noise.

"If Cynthia's there," she said, "Cynthia's talking."

They crept quietly around the house, listening at each downstairs window. Then Marlene climbed up onto the Strongman's shoulders, and they started around again, listening at each upstairs window.

They were in luck almost at once.

"But, Cynthia," came a voice, "how will we know if Jonathan really *is* guilty or not?"

"Ah, my dear Kevin," came the answer, "I have a fiendishly clever plan."

Out in the darkness, the Twisty Lady smiled grimly.

"All I do is say the words 'Morning Glory Machine,' and if he's guilty, he'll jump or turn pale or begin to babble, 'It wasn't me—they made me do it—it's not my fault.' They always do something like that. It never fails. I propose to put him to the test someplace where he'll be completely unsuspecting, such as during breakfast or maybe crossing the street to school. Yes. Crossing the street to school. Perfect."

There was a short, satisfied pause.

"Cynthia," came the voice, "I think you're wonderful! But isn't there anything *I* can do?"

"You, Kevin, are the most important of all," Cynthia replied. "Without *you,* the plan has no hope of succeeding. Your job is to keep the real crossing guard—"

"Who, Mrs. Stopper?"

"Yes—*you* must keep Mrs. Stopper busy while *I* pretend to be the crossing guard and trap Jonathan."

"I could maybe get her talking," said Kevin. "She has sore feet, you know. Or maybe . . ."

Cynthia's voice became warm and furry.

"Thank you, Kevin," she said. "I knew I could count on you. Now, let's get some sleep. Oh, and tomorrow . . ."

"H'm?" murmured Kevin.

"We must tell your parents something. About me."

Outside, the Twisty Lady climbed down from the Strongman's shoulders. Then, unseen in the night, they crept silently away.

CHAPTER 7

Wallawalla Bing Bong

Wednesday morning dawned clear and hopeful. Cynthia, however, was embarrassed to find that she had *no* crossing guard disguise in her suitcase.

"Closest thing I have," she said, "would be Number 333. Pumpkin disguise."

"Never mind," said Kevin. "I can tell you where Mrs. Stopper keeps her vest and sign and stuff at school. But what are we going to tell my mom and dad about *you?*"

"I've given it some thought," said Cynthia. "No problem."

Turning to the suitcase, she pulled out a big hat with a wide brim and some khaki shorts.

"Disguise Number 987," she said proudly. "Australian exchange student from Wallawalla Bing Bong."

If anything could make a kangaroo look more Australian than she did already, this was it. Still, as they went downstairs together, Kevin was worried. As they reached the kitchen door, he stopped. There was no denying that Cynthia could be a little overpowering, at least to begin with. His parents weren't expecting anything. . . .

"Let me go in first," he whispered anxiously to his friend. "O.K.?"

Cynthia winked.

"No prob, Kev," she whispered back.

Strangely, this did not make him feel any better.

What *were* his parents going to think?

Kevin opened the door and took a deep breath.

"Er, Mom," he began, "Dad, I'd like you to meet—"

"BRUCE!" Cynthia exploded into the room. "BRUCE BY NAME AND BRUCE BY TRADE, SPORT! I CAN'T TELL YOU HOW FAN-DINKUM-TASTIC

IT IS OF YOU TO HAVE ME TO STAY, ALL THE WAY FROM WALLAWALLA BING BONG! MY MATE KEV HERE IS MUCH OBLIGED, TOO! WHAT'S FOR BREAKFAST?!"

Kevin, Kevin's mom, and Kevin's dad gulped. The loudest thing that had ever happened in their kitchen before had been the odd bit of toast popping up. Cynthia (or Bruce) was more like an emergency landing of a Concorde jet.

And it kept on, right through breakfast.

"DID YOU HEAR THE ONE ABOUT THE KANGAROO WHO WANTED TO GET RID OF HIS OLD BOOMER-ANG? YEAH, HE THREW IT DOWN A ONE-WAY STREET! GET IT? A ONE-WAY STREET! BOOM-BOOM-BOOMERANG! WALTZING MATIL-DINKUM-DA!"

Bruce told them all about Australia, about the mighty koala herds that roam the outback, about the flocks of flying wallabies, and the ferocious giant platy-puses that lurk along the billabongs.

Kevin's parents were spellbound.

Bruce told them about the Annual All-Australia Joke Festival. People traveled hundreds of miles to hear old favorites like—

What do you do with a green kangaroo? You wait till it ripens. BOOM-BOOM!
Or—

What do you do with a blue kangaroo? You try to cheer it up. BOOM-BOOM!

And then there were the brand-new jokes, never heard before by a living soul. Bruce said comics worked in secret for months on these and that there were prizes for the best ones.

"AND DO THE PEOPLE LAUGH? I'LL SAY! YOU WOULDN'T CATCH A KOOKABURRA LAUGHING ANY HARDER. CRIKEY, LOOK AT THE TIME! BETTER GET GOING, KEV. G'DAY AND THANKS A BUNDLE!"

And Bruce was gone, a dazed Kevin stumbling after.

In the sudden quiet, Kevin's mom and dad looked at each other.

"What . . . what a nice boy," said Kevin's mom.

"Yes . . . yes . . . and so . . . um . . . outgoing," said Kevin's dad.

"Very! Imagine us forgetting he was coming," murmured Kevin's mom.

"Maybe he'll get our Kevin to be less quiet," murmured Kevin's dad. He gave himself a shake. "Crikey, look at the time!"

"To work!" said Kevin's mom with a smile.

CHAPTER 8

Cross-Purposes

Mrs. Stopper, the crossing guard, was just coming out of her house. As she locked the front door, she couldn't help groaning a little. Her feet were killing her. Mrs. Stopper didn't hold with complaining in public, but she allowed herself a moan or two when she was alone.

"Er, hello, Mrs. Stopper," came a voice.

"Aaaaghhh!" gargled Mrs. Stopper. "I didn't know there was anyone there!" Then she peered about, confused. "Is there? Anyone there? Where?"

"Er, here," came the voice, and Kevin stepped out from behind a bush.

Mrs. Stopper collapsed on her front step in relief and surprise. Of course, she knew all the children at school, but Kevin was one of the quiet ones. She'd barely heard him speak before. She couldn't imagine him saying boo to a goose, but here he was, on her doorstep, scaring the living daylights out of her!

"Can I help you, Kevin?" she asked weakly.

Kevin shook his head and brought a cardboard box out from behind his back.

"No, Mrs. Stopper," he said, "but I think *I* can help *you.*"

He sat down on the step beside her and opened the box.

"Look," he said with a shy smile. "I invented these for you."

Mrs. Stopper peered inside. She saw a pair of large, fluffy, soothingly soft . . . *somethings.* She looked at Kevin, puzzled.

"Marshmallow Trampoline Super Slippers," he said. "Your size."

• • • • • • • • •

A few streets away, Cynthia had slipped into the school without being seen and was carefully following the map Kevin had drawn for her.

"Corridor on the right, third door on the left," she murmured. "Marked THE OFFICE. Hat, sign, orange vest on hooks inside, by the door. Aha!"

She stood completely still for a moment, took a deep breath, then grabbed the doorknob and lunged into the room.

"Mrs. Stopper's been delayed—I'm the substitute crossing guard—Thank you—Bye!" she said all in one breath.

"H'm?" said the principal, looking up, but whoever had spoken was already gone, as were Mrs. Stopper's hat, sign, and bright orange vest.

"Fine, fine," murmured the principal and returned to the accounts.

• • • • • • • • •

"There she is," hissed the Strongman. He was feeling extremely uncomfortable in a dress several sizes too small for him, and the scarf he'd tied around his head kept slipping over his eyes. He'd complained to Marlene, but the Twisty Lady had no sympathy for him. If *he* thought being folded up in a *baby carriage* was a *picnic,* she'd snarled, then he was welcome to try it.

"O.K., as we planned," Marlene whispered now. "You make the grab and stuff her in here with me. I'll wrap around her and make sure she doesn't escape. And will you *please* stop squirming like that! Especially as *some* of us don't have *room* to squirm!"

The Strongman stopped squirming, started pushing the carriage, and then stopped that, too.

"She's taking someone else across," he whispered. "We'll have to wait."

● ● ● ● ● ● ● ● ●

Cynthia was feeling extremely pleased with herself. She knew she looked good in orange, and her very first customer of the day was the one person she most wanted to see—Jonathan the paperboy. It was all she could do to keep her feet on the ground. She guided the suspect gently as far as the middle of the road and then sprang her trap.

"Morning Glory Machine!" she cried and watched keenly for her victim's guilty response.

In vain.

Not only did Jonathan not jump or grow pale or babble wildly or react in any guilty sort of way, he didn't react *at all.* By the time Cynthia had escorted him safely to the other side of the street, she knew he could not be the thief.

"He's innocent," she murmured to herself. "No motive."

It seemed pretty obvious that Jonathan already *knew* how to go well into the morning without waking up.

"You've no need for a Morning Glory Machine, have you?" said Cynthia, to which Jonathan replied in a dreamy voice, "No toast today, please, Mom," and wandered on his way.

(If Cynthia had had x-ray vision, she would have realized that she was only partly right about this. In spite of his skills at sleepwalking, Jonathan *did* need a Morning Glory Machine, if only to get his underpants on the right way around.)

Oh, well, never mind, thought Cynthia. She bustled back across the street to help her second customer of the day, an unusually large mother with a baby carriage.

"OOOchee-KOOchee-KOO!" Cynthia said, bending over to look at the baby. She only wanted to be friendly. She just forgot about her tail. She certainly didn't *mean* to trip up the unusually large mother. And how was she to know the carriage would go rolling off down the sidewalk like that and tip over into a bush?

Just then, Kevin whistled. It was the signal they'd agreed upon, to warn Cynthia that Mrs. Stopper was coming.

Cynthia was torn. She wanted to go and help the large mother get the baby carriage out of the bush, but she also needed to get her crossing guard things back before Mrs. Stopper arrived.

Fortunately, when she looked again, she saw that her help wasn't needed.

The baby was already halfway out of the carriage and throwing rattles and bits of bush at its mother.

Couldn't do that if it were hurt, thought Cynthia with relief and bounded off.

She raced into the now-busy school and crashed past a secretary, three students, and a book cart. "Corridor on right, third door on left, oops, sorry, can't stop." She skidded through the door marked THE OFFICE.

"Mrs. Stopper's back—Thanks a lot—Bye!"

"H'm?" said the principal, but the substitute crossing guard was gone again, leaving the sign, the hat, and the bright orange vest swaying gently on their hooks.

"Fine, fine," the principal murmured.

CHAPTER 9

Big Bush, Little Bush

When Kevin's mom and dad came down to breakfast on Thursday morning, they were surprised to see two bushes, one large and one small, eating cereal at the kitchen table.

"Er, Kevin?" said his dad.

"Bruce? Is that you?" said Kevin's mom.

But the bushes had no time to chat.

"Sorry, Mom, gotta run."

"G'DAY! G'DAY! IT'S TIME TO LEAF! HA, HA! GET IT? LEAF?"

"Look, here she comes!" said the small bush, dashing for the door.

"AND THERE SHE GOES!" said the big bush, bounding after.

And then there was nothing left but a little spilled milk, a drifting leaf, and the distant sound of dogs barking.

"School play?" said Kevin's mom, dazed.

"Must be," said Kevin's dad, bewildered. "I think we need some coffee."

"I think you're right," said Kevin's mom.

• • • • • • • • •

Meanwhile, Mrs. Trott was having a most peculiar morning. Although her walks with the dogs always *looked* out of control, they followed a very precise pattern. Every day, she and her two dogs took the same route at the same speed at the same time. The dogs sniffed in passing at the same bushes, and Mrs. Trott said hello to the same people, who were out walking *their* dogs or checking on the weather or heading off to work.

But today was different.

For one thing, there must have been some kind of sale on at the garden center. It seemed that everywhere Mrs. Trott looked, people had planted new bushes. The bushes appeared to be exactly the same and always in groups of two, one large and one small. And they were always extremely rustle-y!

The dogs greeted each appearance of the bushes with excited barking, sniffing, and jumping. They dragged Mrs. Trott along with them at high speed.

There was one more strange thing— Mrs. Trott must have said hello to the same two strangers at least *four* times. There was an unusually large woman in a very small dress and a very thin man with a big black mustache. Each time Mrs. Trott was jerked off course by her dogs' interest in new bushes, there the two of them would be. The large woman and the thin man seemed quite embarrassed by it all.

It was really *very* peculiar.

● ● ● ● ● ● ● ● ●

As Mrs. Trott arrived home, even more breathless than usual, the telephone was ringing. She rushed in, leaving the front door open.

"Hello?" she said loudly, for Mrs. Trott was a little deaf. "Oh, it's you, dear. Yes, just back. And what a *morning,* Glori— Pardon me? Oh. Yes, I'd love to meet you for afternoon tea. Four o'clock? The Blue Begonia? Fine. That'll be lovely. Yes. See you then. Bye."

Mrs. Trott hung up the phone and said, "Well, well, well. And doesn't she just know who *else* will be at the Blue Begonia at four o'clock on a Thursday!"

Mrs. Trott shook her head and chuckled. Then she went over to the window to see what the dogs were so excited about.

At first, she couldn't see anything.

Then her eyes traveled upward. She blinked.

"Perhaps I need a vacation," she murmured.

She shut the door and went to take a nice, soothing nap.

● ● ● ● ● ● ● ● ●

Up in the tree, two bushes looked at each other, leaves quivering.

"Did you hear that?" hissed the big bush. "She said, 'Morning Glory.' And 'four o'clock.' And the 'Blue . . . Petunia'? Sounds like code to me."

"She *did!* She really *did!* This has got to be *it!*" whispered the little bush excitedly. "She's going to meet someone and hand over the plans! Except it's the 'Blue Begonia.' That's the café down on Main Street."

"Then *that's* where we've got to be, in time for the handover," said the first bush. "We've got to be right there on the

spot but without arousing anyone's suspicions. Very nervous, these criminal types. One whisker out of place, and the whole thing gets canceled."

"I could go as an ordinary customer," suggested the second bush.

"Cunning plan!" said the first. "But what about *me?* I haven't *got* an ordinary disguise."

"Well," said the second bush slowly, "I heard my mom say that the Blue Begonia is advertising for a new waitress. . . ."

"BUT THAT'S PERFECT!" cried the first bush and then hushed to a whisper. "That's fan-dinkum-tastic! What are we waiting for? *Waiting for?* Get it?"

"Yeah!" The second bush giggled. "Boom-boom! Let's go!"

There was a pause, and for a moment, nothing happened.

Then the first bush said—

"How did the kangaroo get down out

of the tree while dressed in a big bush disguise?"

The second bush thought and then said—

"I don't know. How *did* the kangaroo get down out of the tree while dressed in a big bush disguise?"

"Very, very carefully," said the first bush.

There was another pause. Then—

"Is that a joke?" asked the second bush in a puzzled voice.

"No," said the first bush as it began to edge along the branch. "It's just very good advice."

CHAPTER 10

There's a Kangaroo in My Soup!

Cynthia looked terrific. When Kevin got home from school that afternoon, he found her wearing a little black dress with a white collar and a white frilly apron and a white frilly cap that (almost) hid her ears. She held a menu in one paw and a pad and pencil in the other. Thanks to Disguise Number 76, she looked the perfect waitress.

"Now, remember," said Kevin anxiously, "I'll be there with the pocket tape recorder. You make sure she feels safe. She mustn't think anyone is watching

her. Be careful. Be polite. Don't put your paws in the food—"

"Waiter, waiter, there's a kangaroo in my soup!"

"Sh! Not so loud, or the other customers will be wanting one, too. BOOM-BOOM!"

"And *no jokes*," said Kevin. "Look, just make sure you do exactly as you're told, and you'll be fine."

"No jokes!" muttered Cynthia as she set off for the restaurant. "Be careful! No paws in the food! Do as you're told! This isn't going to be fun *at all!*"

● ● ● ● ● ● ● ● ●

The café was crowded, and the chef was very busy when Cynthia arrived.

"Good!" he barked. "Get started. Table 6 wants this Cream Tea Special for one, and get that boy's order at Table 5."

Cynthia saw Kevin, seated as close to Mrs. Trott and her friend at Table 4 as was humanly possible. She could just see the tape recorder sticking out of his shirt pocket. The setup couldn't be better.

Carrying the tray of Cream Tea Special for one with both paws, Cynthia went to serve Table 6.

"No jokes. No paws in the food. Do exactly as you're told," she murmured to herself. Slowly and carefully, she put the cup and saucer on the table. Slowly and carefully, she put the milk pitcher on the table. Slowly and carefully, she put the teapot on the table. And all the while, she listened intently to Mrs. Trott's conversation with her friend.

"I really do think I'm going rather peculiar, my dear," Mrs. Trott was saying. "Why, just this morning, Glori . . ."

Mrs. Trott's voice trailed off as she noticed the intense brown gaze of the new waitress fixed on her.

Cynthia's heart skipped a beat, and she quickly looked up at the ceiling, trying to appear casual. Morning Glory! Mrs.

Trott had been about to say, "Morning Glory Machine"! Evidence!

The customer at Table 6, an elderly gentleman, decided to help the new waitress unload the tray. Unfortunately, just as he leaned for the sugar, Cynthia, still staring up at the ceiling, leaned toward Mrs. Trott's table to make sure she didn't miss a word.

As Kevin watched, the gentleman's lean turned into more of a *dive*. For a moment, time seemed to slow down. A look of horror spread gradually across the gentleman's face.

The other customers stared, spoons and cups frozen halfway to their mouths, eyes wide. Cynthia's lips began to form the word "Whoops!" Then the moment was over, time and gravity returned to normal, and with a yelp, the gentleman hit the floor nose first.

Mrs. Trott and her friend shrieked and fluttered at him.

"Oh!" they cried. "Matthew Prometheus! Good heavens! Are you all right?"

The man rose with a gallantly suppressed groan.

"Hello, Emily," he said to Mrs. Trott. "Yes, I'm fine. Just an accident."

Then he turned to Mrs. Trott's companion, and his face went all goopy.

"Good morning, Gloria. Sorry to have startled you."

The woman called Gloria blushed right down to her sensible shoes.

"It's . . . it's afternoon," she stuttered.

Mr. Prometheus looked confused. Then he stared down at his feet and murmured, "But . . . when you're around, it always *feels* like morning. A fresh . . . *beautiful* morning."

Shyly, Gloria put a hand on his arm.

"Won't you join us . . . Matthew?" she asked.

Matthew looked longingly at Gloria. Gloria looked sweetly at Matthew. Emily

Trott looked at both of them with a kindly expression.

Cynthia looked at Kevin and put her paw over her mouth. Kevin looked pained and turned off the pocket tape recorder. He wasn't sure which was worse—seeing old people acting mushy or being wrong about Mrs. Trott.

Cynthia collected her tray and drifted back to the kitchen.

The chef, whose face was now an unhealthy shade of purple, met her at the door.

"What took you so long?" he hissed, trying not to be heard by the customers.

Cynthia looked surprised.

"I was just being careful," she said.

"It's all very well being careful," said the chef gruffly, "but you were too slow! Everything will be cold by the time it gets to the tables. Here, take these bowls of soup to Table 3."

Cynthia peered about.

"Which table?" she asked sweetly.

"Table 3," said the chef through clenched teeth. "The table by the door."

Cynthia looked and was astonished. There, sitting at Table 3, was the unusually large mother from yesterday! She seemed to have left the baby at home today and brought its father instead—a thin man who looked amazingly like the baby, except for a large black mustache.

The chef's foot was tapping dangerously.

"*Now*, please," he growled. "And I would appreciate it if you would hop to it."

Cynthia looked at him.

"You can't be serious," she said.

The chef lost his temper and forgot all about trying to be quiet.

"HOP TO IT!" he bellowed.

So Cynthia did.

A woman at Table 2 was just saying to her husband, "I wonder what the soup of the day is?" when some of it hit her on the back of the head. A man wearing glasses at Table 7 yelled, "Help! Who turned out the lights?" Matthew Prometheus cried gallantly, "Fear not, Gloria! I will save you!"

Cynthia hopped on and landed hard at Table 3. The bowls flew gracefully off the tray and landed upside down, with a satisfying *squelch,* on top of the unusually large mother and the tall, thin father.

There was a moment of total stillness. No one moved. There was no sound but the gentle drip of cream of tomato making its way to the floor.

Then, with a roar like an avalanche, the chef began to bellow. The customers began to shout and shriek. And Cynthia, grabbing Kevin on her way past, began to run.

• • • • • • • • •

Halfway down the street, they stopped running. They stood there, panting, and for a moment, Cynthia said nothing.

Then she put a soup-flavored paw on Kevin's shoulder.

"Sometimes," she said solemnly, "it just *isn't* a good idea to do exactly as you're told."

Kevin tried very hard to look serious. He really did try. But he didn't succeed. Little bits of laughter started to escape.

"Did you see," he said with a giggle,

"that man with the soup all over his glasses? And how that other man's mustache nearly came off when the bowl landed on his head and the soup dribbled down and—OOF!"

Kevin was shoved to one side by a man with a briefcase, who hurried past without even saying, "Sorry."

"Well!" said Cynthia indignantly.

"Did you see that?" squeaked Kevin. "He pushed me! Did you see . . ." His voice trailed off as he stared after the man. He grabbed Cynthia's arm and pointed. *"Did you see who that was?"*

"A very rude man?" said Cynthia, peering after him.

"No!" stuttered Kevin. "I mean, yes! I mean, that's the Double-Pane Salesman! The D.P.S.! Suspect Number 3!"

"He's crossing the street!" cried Cynthia.

"He's going into that store!" cried Kevin.

"It's the Everything and Then Some Department Store!" cried Cynthia.

"And there's a sign in the window!" cried Kevin. "And it says . . ."

"CLEANER WANTED!" they cried together.

Kevin and Cynthia looked at each other.

"Disguise Number 62," Cynthia said. "Kevin, I think we're wonderful!"

And Kevin agreed.

CHAPTER 11

Not-So-Quiet Kevin

It was hard for Kevin to pay attention at school the next day. He couldn't help wondering how Cynthia was getting on. He'd left her at home putting the finishing touches on Disguise Number 62, the Cleaning Lady Deluxe.

"I want to be irresistible," she'd said. "I want the store to hire me on the spot! And once I'm in, I'll be waiting when that D.P.S. comes back, and no mistake!!"

Kevin's teacher was also having trouble concentrating, though not for the same reason. The morning was nearly over, and she found herself with nothing particularly planned to teach. She'd finished one topic, and there was no point in starting a new one. Not on a Friday, not just before the lunch break. Whenever this happened, she usually had a session of "What-do-you-want-to-be-when-you-grow-up?" to fill in the time before the bell rang.

And it was usually pretty boring. The whole class slumped in their chairs and glazed over. Everybody always knew exactly what everybody else was going to say. Gregory always said he wanted to be an astronaut. Amy always said she wanted to be a world-famous, very rich, downhill skier. Melissa always said she wanted to be a pig farmer. Quiet Kevin always said he wanted to be an inventor like his mom and dad. Yawn. Come to think of it, it was Kevin's turn right now.

"And what would you like to be when you grow up, Kevin?" droned his teacher.

Kevin wasn't listening. His mind was far away, with Cynthia.

"Kevin?" said his teacher, a little louder.

"Um? Oh?" said Kevin, coming back with a jerk. "Er. A kangaroo."

There was a pause. The class sat up a little.

"When you grow up, you want to be a . . . *kangaroo?*" said his teacher. What had come over Quiet Kevin?

"No, ma'am," said Kevin. "I still want to be a great inventor. But"—his voice shook a little, yet he carried on—"I also want to be a kangaroo . . . comic." The class sat up a bit more. "Somebody who stands up and tells kangaroo jokes. Like this."

His hands were trembling, and he felt icy cold all over. Nevertheless, Quiet Kevin walked up to the front of the class and said in a loud, clear voice—

"What do you get if you cross a kangaroo with an elephant?"

"I don't know," said his teacher weakly. "What *do* you get if you cross a kangaroo with an elephant?"

"Great big holes all over Australia!"

There was a moment of horrible silence. Then Kevin remembered.

"BOOM-BOOM!" he said.

And it happened.

First there was a giggle from the back. Then a snort from over by the window. Everybody was sitting up now. There were grins all over the place. Even Kevin's teacher was smiling!

Kevin stopped feeling quite so icy cold. He started feeling a little warm and pink.

"What do you call a lazy baby kangaroo?" he said.

"We don't know!" called someone from the back of the class.

"A pouch potato. BOOM-BOOM!" said Kevin.

It happened again! And at that

moment, Kevin felt toasty right down to his toes.

"Who do you think invented the kangaroo?"

Kevin loved this one.

"Who did, Kevin? Who invented the kangaroo?" everyone shouted.

"Somebody with a canning factory and loads of Garoos!"

There was a longer pause while one half of the class explained the joke to the other half, and someone near the front explained it to the teacher.

Then everyone yelled, *"BOOM-BOOM!"*

"More, Kevin, more!" chanted his class.

Even Kevin's teacher asked, "*Do* you know any more kangaroo jokes?"

Kevin smiled.

"I know a million!"

Cynthia would be proud of me! he thought.

CHAPTER 12

The Everything and Then Some Department Store

And Cynthia *would* have been proud of Kevin, if she hadn't at that very moment been extremely busy.

Lavinia Humble, the Assistant Manager of the Everything and Then Some Department Store, was not sure what had hit her. She didn't usually hire staff just like that, on the spot, but when Cynthia (disguised as Mrs. Cynthia Hoover) arrived, asking about the cleaner's job, Lavinia had found her strangely irresistible.

Maybe it was Mrs. Hoover's enthusiasm? She certainly seemed eager.

For example, when Lavinia said, "Please, if you don't mind, that is, I was wondering if, perhaps, you wouldn't mind dusting in the China Department . . . ?"

"Mind? MIND?" Cynthia cried. "That would be terrific! I *love* dusting! Yessiree Bob!"

Which was all well and good, but you couldn't deny that *some* things about the new cleaner were rather peculiar.

For one thing, she *muttered*. Lavinia could hear her whispering away as she worked, saying things like "And no hopping!" and "Come out, come out, wherever you are!" and "Where can you be, little D.P.S.?"

What was that all about?

And then there was the strange way that Mrs. Hoover, well, *pounced*. She'd be dusting along very carefully, and then out of the blue, she'd leap behind a display cabinet shouting, "A-HA!" or "Gotcha!" Of course, there wouldn't be

anybody there, and then she'd pretend she'd just been sneezing. "AH-*CHOO!*" Every time she did this, Lavinia jumped nervously and went "OH!" The customers did, too.

Not surprisingly, the China Department emptied fast. Except, that is, for two customers, a man and a woman, who were wearing big coats, dark glasses, and hats pulled down low over their eyes.

Lavinia went up to them.

"May I help you?" she said.

The two customers began talking at the same time.

"No, thank you. We're just browsing," said the woman.

"Yeah, we're looking for this kangar—OW!" said the man.

The woman had kicked him.

"A-HA! AH-*CHOO!*" said Cynthia, appearing suddenly at Lavinia's elbow. "All done here! What's next?"

"OH!" Lavinia jumped. "Ah." She turned back to excuse herself to the customers, but they had disappeared without saying good-bye.

Lavinia Humble felt quite frazzled.

Cynthia winked, as if to reassure her, but strangely, this did not make Lavinia feel better.

"Would you mind vacuuming?" Lavinia quavered. "In the Toy Department?"

"Vacuuming! Great!" cried Cynthia. "If there's anything I like better than dusting, it's vacuuming! Show me the way!"

It wasn't easy for Lavinia to tell if the strange Mrs. Hoover was still muttering, because of the noise from the vacuum cleaner. But she was definitely still pouncing.

The Assistant Manager spent a frantic half-hour rescuing teddy bears, capturing runaway trains, and restacking building blocks. All the customers ran away, though most of the children didn't want to and had to be dragged by their parents.

The only ones who remained were the man and the woman in dark glasses. It was strange how they kept hanging about in the Toy Department. And, even stranger, they seemed to be trying to get *closer* to the new cleaner.

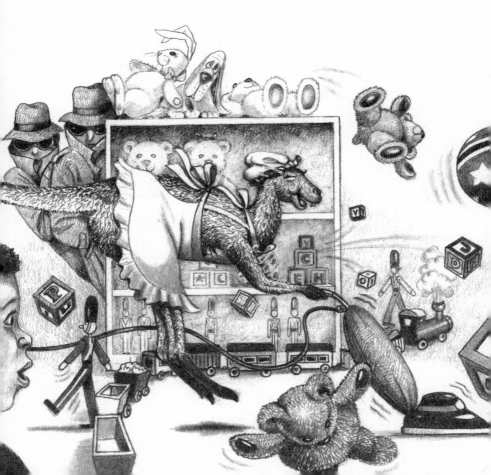

"Hello. May I be of assistance?" Lavinia called loudly over the vacuum's roar.

"Yeah!" bellowed the man. "We want to know, is that cleaning lady a kangar— OUCH!"

The woman had kicked him again.

"Only looking," she yelled and dragged the big man away just as Cynthia switched off the vacuum cleaner.

Quiet. How wonderful, thought Lavinia.

It didn't last very long.

"All spick and span here!" chirped Mrs. Hoover loudly. "Where to now?"

At that moment, one of the store clerks came up to Lavinia.

"Excuse me, Ms. Humble," he said politely, "but we're having some trouble in the Beds Department."

"Oh dear," sighed Lavinia. "Not the Adjusto-Bed, Peter?"

"I'm afraid so," said Peter. "It's making funny noises again."

"Did you say Adjusto-Bed?" interrupted Cynthia excitedly. "As in Extra-Special Supercharged Motorized Computerized Adjusto-Bed, Mark 6?"

"Why, yes," said Peter in surprise.

"But that's amazing!" Cynthia cried. "I've always wanted to have a look at one of those! It's making funny noises, you say?"

"Oh dear, oh my, I don't think . . . ," quavered Lavinia, but it was too late. Cynthia and Peter were already on their way.

"I really should go, too," Lavinia said to herself. "It really would be unworthy of my position as Assistant Manager not to go, too. I really should go."

She took a deep breath, coughed nervously, and headed for the Beds Department.

● ● ● ● ● ● ● ● ●

At the doorway to the Beds Department, Lavinia came to an abrupt stop. She froze. And gulped. And stared. Never in her twelve and a half years as Assistant Manager of the Everything and Then Some Department Store had she seen anything like this.

The new cleaner and Peter, the store clerk, were bent over the control box at the back of the Adjusto-Bed. Sneaking up on them in a most suspicious manner were the two mysterious customers in dark glasses. It looked as if they were just about to jump on Cynthia Hoover, when Peter said, "It's this button here, I think."

And he pushed it.

At once the mysterious customers were scooped up by the bed, stuffed into a comforter cover, thrown onto the mattress, and plumped up. Muffled shrieks and cries for help rang out in the Beds Department.

Cynthia and Peter, busy with the control box, looked at one another, puzzled.

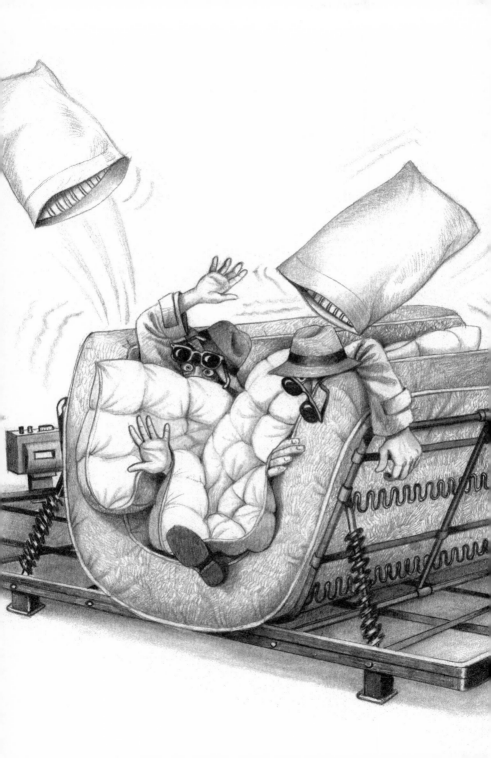

"It certainly does make funny noises," said Cynthia. "What happens when you push this button?"

She pushed it, and immediately the bed began to shudder enthusiastically. The shrieks turned to gargles, then giggles, then guffaws.

"It's getting worse!" cried Peter in alarm.

"You're right!" said Cynthia. "There's only one thing left to do. I'm going to reboot the boogle wart. No time to argue. Here goes!"

Peter gasped and hid his eyes as Cynthia thrust a paw right into the back of the bed and pulled. The mysterious strangers were thrown out of the bed, through the air, and into a nearby laundry basket. The Adjusto-Bed gave a bleat like an anguished sheep. And everything was still.

Lavinia Humble stood in the doorway, a look of horror on her face. Oblivious to all, Cynthia and Peter were talking eagerly together about control boxes and contrary motion. The strangers picked themselves out of the laundry basket and staggered away. And the Extra-Special Supercharged Motorized Computerized Adjusto-Bed, Mark 6, sat there, smug and silent.

"Oh dear," moaned Lavinia. "Oh dear, oh dear."

Cynthia looked up.

"Oh, there you are!" she boomed cheerfully. "My goodness, you look all worn out! I think you've done quite enough for one morning. See you later, Pete! What you need," she said to Lavinia, as she led her out of the Beds Department and toward the staff room, "is a lovely cup of tea and one of my homemade jokes."

Lavinia smiled weakly.

"Just the tea," she whispered.

But Cynthia knew better. As the kettle boiled, she began—

"Which kangaroo can jump higher than a house?"

She got no further. The intercom buzzed on, and a rude voice shouted, "Humble! Two coffees. Now!" Then the intercom buzzed off.

Lavinia moaned.

"It's Mr. Boar, the Manager," she babbled, desperately trying to tidy herself and make coffee at the same time. "He's a rude, horrid man—"

"He certainly is," said Cynthia.

"And he's always trying to fire me—"

"The brute," said Cynthia.

"And I know he'll have that awful Double-Pane Salesman with him. The store already *has* double-pane windows, but he's always in there with Mr. Boar, and I don't *like* him—" A tear trickled down her nose.

"LAVINIA HUMBLE," said Cynthia in her lion-tamer's voice. "SIT!" (Though Cynthia had never actually tamed lions at the circus, she'd listened very carefully.)

Lavinia sat.

"BLOW YOUR NOSE!" said Cynthia.

Lavinia blew.

"STAY!" said Cynthia.

There was a feeble "But—" from Lavinia, but she stayed.

Cynthia grabbed the coffee tray and headed for Mr. Boar's office.

CHAPTER 13

Coffee Can Be Bad for Your Health

Cynthia knocked on the door.

"What?" the rude voice shouted.

"Coffee, sir," said Cynthia sweetly.

"Get in here!" shouted the voice, and Cynthia got.

There they were, standing by the desk—Mr. Boar the Manager and the Double-Pane Salesman. The two men stared suspiciously at Cynthia.

"Who do you think *you* are?" said Mr. Boar.

"The new cleaner, sir," said Cynthia.

"I've brought your coffee, sir. Ms. Humble was not feeling well. Sir."

Mr. Boar grunted.

"I should fire that woman," he said, and then he glared at Cynthia, daring her to say a word. She didn't. He grunted again.

"Black, no sugar," he said. He glared at the Double-Pane Salesman. "And *he* takes milk and enough sugar to make a cat sick."

Mr. Boar believed in being rude to *everybody.*

Over by the window, Cynthia began to pour the coffee. Mr. Boar was already talking to the D.P.S. as if she weren't there.

"Are you sure you copied the *final* drawings?" he said. "I don't want another mess-up like last time, when you brought me the plans for the Underwater Shower before they'd even finished work on it! Idiot!"

"Oh yes, sir," whined the Double-Pane Salesman. "Satisfaction guaranteed, sir!

I overheard them saying to each other, 'Well, that's it, then. The Morning Glory Machine is ready to be made. Our best invention ever!' So I climbed in through the window and copied the drawings and—"

"You'd better be right," interrupted Mr. Boar. "Now, what's this part supposed to be?"

As the two men bent over the plans, Cynthia crept closer. Her eyes were bright, her nose was twitching, and she held a large cup of extremely hot coffee in each paw. Quietly she put a cup on each chair. Carefully she moved each chair to a point exactly behind each man. Silently she smiled. Then . . .

"SIT!" said Cynthia in her lion-tamer's voice.

And they sat.

As Mr. Boar and the D.P.S. roared and leaped about the room holding their bottoms, Cynthia grabbed the plans for

the Morning Glory Machine and raced
for the door.

CHAPTER 14

Stop, Thief!

It was twelve noon on the dot as Mack's Circus came rolling down Main Street. The Ringmaster peered angrily from side to side, trying to spot the Twisty Lady and the Strongman.

"And they better well and truly have that kangaroo with them," he muttered fiercely, "or else fur is going to fly."

Nobody felt it was a good moment to point out to him that neither Marlene nor Fred *had* fur. This was wise, because wisps of steam had already started to come out of the Ringmaster's ears.

They had just stopped at the light by a big department store, when one of the Ringing Brothers gasped.

"Look, Boss!"

A tangle of bodies came tumbling out of the store's big front door. One struggled to its feet and set off down the street, a bunch of papers clutched in one paw.

"It's her!" cried the Ringmaster. "I'd know that tail anywhere! AFTER HER!"

Leaving the circus van right in the middle of the street, the Ringmaster and his performers piled out and headed off after Cynthia. Meanwhile, the bodies on the sidewalk had sorted themselves into Marlene, Fred, the Double-Pane Salesman, and Mr. Boar. Lavinia Humble peered out anxiously from the doorway. They joined the chase, one and all.

"Stop that kangaroo!" yelled the Ringmaster.

"Stop that cleaning lady!" bellowed Mr. Boar.

"Stop that thief!" shouted the D.P.S.

"Oh dear, oh dear," whimpered Lavinia.

"Wait for us!" cried Fred and Marlene.

"Kevvvinnnnn!" wailed Cynthia.

The lunch bell had just rung as the chase swept past the school. Without waiting for the crossing guard, Kevin raced recklessly across the street, yelling, "Cynthia! Cynthia!"

"Kevin! Come back here!" cried Mrs. Stopper. "You can't cross a street like that! It's dangerous! Come back here, and do it properly!" She bounded after him like an elderly, pumpkin-colored gazelle. Her sore feet meant nothing to her now that she was wearing Marshmallow Trampoline Super Slippers.

Mrs. Trott was walking her dogs home from their annual visit to the vet.

"What's that noise?" she asked, but the dogs didn't care about the noise. They had caught a whiff of the wonderful bushes from yesterday, or if not the bushes, then something very like them.

They were off! Cutting through several gardens and a goldfish pond, the dogs and their mistress galloped, hot on the trail. The dogs were barking wildly, and Mrs. Trott was gasping, "Oh! Oh! Oh!"

Kevin's mom and dad were having a quiet chat with Officer MacAngus in the front yard.

"I was a quiet kid myself, you know," Officer MacAngus was saying.

Then an odd roaring sound interrupted him. It seemed to be coming closer. And closer. AND CLOSER!

"I say, I say," said Officer MacAngus. "I say, I—"

But before he was able to say anything,

a large, furry cleaning lady knocked him over and sat on him.

A crowd of red-faced people came panting up behind.

"You . . . you . . . ," growled the Ringmaster.

"Stop, thief!" gasped the Double-Pane Salesman.

"Stop, thief!" puffed Mr. Boar the Manager.

Cynthia looked surprised.

"But I've *stopped* the thieves!" she cried, waving the plans about.

Kevin arrived calling, "Cynthia! Cynthia!" and Mrs. Stopper arrived calling, "Kevin! Kevin!" They were closely followed by a damp and draggled Mrs. Trott. Mrs. Trott's dogs leaped about barking and licking everyone. Then came Lavinia Humble, patting her face with a lace-edged hanky. Marlene and Fred were the last to arrive, looking nervous and mussed-up.

It was pandemonium.

Then Officer MacAngus took charge. From underneath Cynthia, he bellowed, "QUIET!"

And, amazingly, they were. Everyone stopped hollering. Even the dogs stopped barking, sat down, and let their tongues hang out.

Officer MacAngus spoke. "You're squishing me," he said to Cynthia.

"You're welcome," said Cynthia. She got off and helped him up.

Meanwhile, Kevin was trying to get his parents' attention.

"Look, Mom," he panted, "Dad. It's your—" He had no breath left. He grabbed the papers from Cynthia's paw and shoved them at his bewildered parents.

"Just look!"

There was an awful pause as they looked. Then their eyes got bigger. And bigger!

"Hang on a minute—," said Kevin's dad.

"But these are—," said Kevin's mom.

"These are the plans for our Morning Glory Machine!" they cried together.

"Our new invention! It's so new, it hasn't even been made yet!"

There was another moment's silence, broken only by the muffled sounds of many people trying to be out of breath without making any noise about it. Officer MacAngus straightened his jacket.

"H'm," he said, looking at Cynthia with a stern eye. "*You're* a suspicious-looking character! Where did you get these plans?"

"From him!" said Cynthia, pointing at Mr. Boar.

Officer MacAngus turned and looked sternly at Mr. Boar.

"I got them from *him!*" squeaked Mr. Boar, pointing at the Double-Pane Salesman.

Everyone turned and looked sternly at the Double-Pane Salesman.

"Uh-oh," said the D.P.S.

CHAPTER 15

The Last Laugh

After that, nothing was quite the same.

The Double-Pane Salesman and Mr. Boar were arrested by Officer Mac-Angus, which was very exciting for him as he had never had to arrest anyone before. He also gave the Ringmaster a ticket for bad parking.

The Ringmaster grumbled, but paid. Then he took Cynthia to one side.

"If I change the bill," he said gruffly, not quite looking at her, "if I change it so that it says—

Cynthia the Kangaroo
Mistress of a Thousand Disguises
AND
Stand-Up Comic

—then would you come back? The circus isn't the same without you."

"Ringmaster!" exclaimed Cynthia, and she gave him a big, wet kangaroo kiss.

She looked over at Kevin and winked.

Kevin was just standing there quietly, and inside he was feeling sad. I'll never see Cynthia again, he was thinking.

Cynthia turned back to the Ringmaster.

"I'd love to return," she said, "on one condition. I'll need a part-time assistant."

The Ringmaster said, "A *what?*" and Kevin's eyes got big.

"A part-time assistant," said Cynthia. "To help me tell jokes. Every summer vacation. Otherwise . . ."

She winked at Kevin again as the Ringmaster grudgingly agreed. And this time, her wink made Kevin feel MUCH better!

Ms. Humble was feeling better, too. With Mr. Boar out of the way, she could at last become Manager of the Everything and Then Some Department Store, something she had longed to be for every moment of the last twelve and a half years.

She turned to Kevin's mom and dad.

"I'd like to, that is . . . if you don't mind," she began to quaver.

Then she remembered her new position. She took a deep breath and said firmly, "I'd like to order 120 Morning Glory Machines to sell at the store. Just as soon as they are made."

Kevin's mom and dad were very happy. They invited as many people as would fit into their kitchen for milk and cookies. For a while, it was almost as noisy as when Bruce was visiting.

But then there was a quiet moment, and Manager Lavinia said, "There's just one thing I still don't understand."

"What's that, dear?" asked Kevin's mom. "Is it the sprocket pocket? Or the bits that go *blarp?*"

"No," said Lavinia. "It's not about the Morning Glory Machine. It's . . . which kangaroo *can* jump higher than a house?"

Everyone looked confused, and Lavinia blushed.

"It was something Cynthia said," she stuttered. "Before . . . all this. She said, 'Which kangaroo can jump higher than a house?'"

A huge grin spread over Cynthia's furry face, and Kevin said, "I know! I know!"

"Take it away, Kev!" cried Cynthia.

Proudly and loudly, Quiet Kevin said—

"Which kangaroo can jump higher than a house?"

And everybody said, "We don't know! Which kangaroo *can* jump higher than a house?"

Kevin said—

"Any kangaroo. How many houses do you know that can jump?"

He looked at Cynthia. Cynthia looked at him. And they both cried—

"BOOM-BOOM!"

Jokes? I Know a Million!

How do you get a baby kangaroo to go to sleep on the Moon?

Rocket.

What's the difference between a kangaroo and an egg?

Have you ever tried scrambling a kangaroo?

Why did the kangaroo jump up and down?

He'd taken some medicine and forgotten to shake the bottle.

What do kangaroos have that no other animal has?

Baby kangaroos.

What do you call a kangaroo at the North Pole?

Lost.

How do you make a kangaroo float?
Put a scoop of ice cream in a glass of root beer, and add one kangaroo.

How did the kangaroo feel after he ate a pillow?
Down in the mouth.

What do you call a cheerful kangaroo?
A hoptimist.

First Kangaroo: Where's your baby?
Second Kangaroo: My goodness—my pocket's been picked!

What do you get if you cross a kangaroo with a hippopotamus?
Flat Australians.

How do you get a kangaroo to fly?
Buy it an airline ticket.